# Learning English the Cultural Way

# Learning English the Cultural Way

written by and photographs by

## Gail A. Mitchell

Africana Homestead Legacy Publishers
Cherry Hill, New Jersey

**Published by**

Africana Homestead Legacy Publishers
811 Church Road, Suite 105
Cherry Hill, New Jersey 08002
USA

Visit us at www.ahlpub.com or send inquiries to editors@ahlpub.com
For information on ordering copies e-mail book-orders@ahlpub.com

Printed on permanent/durable acid-free paper and bound in the United States of America.
11 10 09 08 07 06 05 04      5 4 3 2 1

Library of Congress Control Number  2004109967
ISBN  0-9653308-9-3 (ISBN-13: 978-0-9653308-9-3)

Photography by Gail Mitchell and AHLP Communications,
an affiliate of Africana Homestead Legacy Publishers.
Special thanks to E. Lama Wonkeryor, Ph.D., AHLP Communications, for his assistance in our
photo shoot.

Carolyn C. Williams  edited, created the typography, designed the graphic elements
of the illustrations, and produced this book.

## Dedicated to

Mitch
Ethelynde H. Williams
Levi D. Johnson
Gladys and Bill Mitchell
Jamal
Janel
Sharon
LaVerne
Bro
Littleone
Bernice
Kevin

**We**
are all new to the U.S.A.
We like very much to learn and play.
Our parents work for different companies,
while we learn English and to cross our Ts.

City
and suburb are where we live,
in apartments, projects, and big houses.
We miss those far away – friends and families,
some who speak Spanish, Russian, or Chinese.

**Ears,**
    **eyes, voices, and growing hands**
**help us learn the culture of our new land.**

**ESL is an important class.**

**We hear, speak, and write English to pass.**

# Our

## next grade level has new teachers

### who expect us to know American features—

Valley Forge * Thomas Jefferson* Independence Hall

Plymouth Rock * Crispus Attucks * Boson Tea Party

Betsy Ross * Benjamin Franklin * Dolly Madison

Thomas  Alva Edison * ¼ ± = > * George Washington Carver

## science, math, and social studies—
## as if our families lived here for centuries.

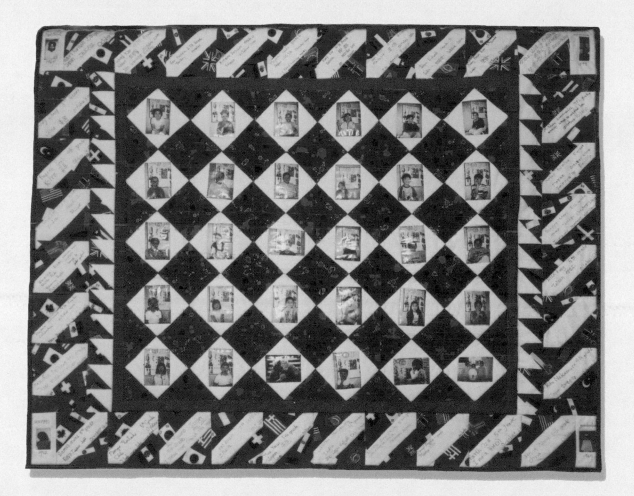

In
ESL class we practice TPR—
total physical response – even with a guitar.

Point, touch, stand, sit, open, close, move around,
we even hear sounds from famous Motown.

Every
month we learn something new.

We will share our new knowledge with you.

In September we learn about our school—

check music, computers, cafeteria — in our gym shoes.

# October

its Tainos, Columbus Day, Halloween.

We make hardcover books in between.

Changing pumpkins to Jack-o-lanterns

Scooping seeds— giggling— 'til our sides burn.

November
we give thanks for our life in America
and learn about maize and Sacajawea.

We ask our families about our histories
and make videotapes to share the stories.

# December
we talk about favorite holidays.

Our families are in the shopping phase.

Hanukkah, Christmas, and then it's Kwanzaa.

Eating latkes, singing carols, shouting AMANDLA!

# January

brings us a brand new year.

We learn about freedom, loud and clear.

We honor Dr. King for his selfless fights
for all Americans to gain their civil rights.

# February

more African American history events
then days for Valentines and presidents.

We draw and write in our ESL books
and read aloud in different classroom nooks.

# March

we honor women, our moms and others,

We find out about sisters – not our brothers!

Green is St. Patrick's day, Purim a joyous thing.

Iranian New Year is the first day of spring.

# April

brings spring into our ESL class.

We travel America on Dad's frequent flyer pass.

Visits to Hawaii, Disney and Washington, D.C.

In ESL we learn about liberty.

**May**

has Mom's very special day.

And we learn English in a special way.

We get Mom's photo, favorite recipe, and song

then write a poem in her honor, so very long.

32

June,
    the hot month, is special for Dad.

We learn to machine sew on a special pad.

Six nine patches — each one about Pop.

His name, his job, even an old tie or sock.

34

# It
takes time to sew and bind it together,

with needle and thread in the hot weather.

We surprise Dad with a song and a party.

He comes with our family to eat very heartily.

Sharing
stories, speaking English every day
helps us keep our culture and learn America's way.

Improving our English as the school year ends,
we'll learn even more when we start school again.

# About the Author

Gail Mitchell is a native New Jerseyan who hails from Newark and East Orange. She graduated from Trenton State College and began her teaching career in the East Orange public school system. She has a master's degree in TESOL, teaches English to speakers of other languages, and has taught ESL to adults as well as children. Among her hobbies are speaking Spanish, biking, and writing poetry. She also plays a mean game of ping pong! Gail Mitchell started quilting in 1989. This is her first book.

# Acknowledgments

This book has been made possible, first and foremost, by the support of the parents and guardians of my English language learners and the enthusiastic thirst for learning of my students from many countries of the world.

I especially want to acknowledge the wisdom, foresight and insight of the following administrators and supervisors, in both the New Brunswick School District and the West Windsor Plains-boro School District, as well as Contra County Community College in Oakland, California. They include Dr. Intisar Shareef, Dr. Penelope Lattimer, Joan Bornheimer, Principal George Buono, Kay Gross, Mary Ann Isaacs, Dianne Gallo, David Lieberman, Sue Di Donato, Rose Miller, Dr. Selma Goore, Diane Taylor, Alicia Boyko, Marcy Rubin, Dr. Barbara Tedesco and Ann Breitman.

Kudos to the following teachers who have been special supporters, ostentatiously and surreptitiously over the years: Tommie Shider, Leslie Katz, Steve Macy, Harriet Karvasarsky, Lynn Grodnick, Deborah Stovall, Jane Cox, Marcey Mandell, Donna Gil, Lori Haas, Carole Herscheit, Theresa Rivera, Mary Santiago, Angela Tran, Janice Chai, Suzy Zhao, Inja Chang, Karen Krech, Connie Beadle, Mickey Mears, Brenda Graham, Michelle Pellecchia, Ronnie Epstein, Carol Watchler, Lynn Holman, Debbie Di Colo and Martha Liebman. A special shout out to the "Trailer Teachers & Friends" group who give that *EXTRA SPECIAL LEARNING* : Sandra Blackstone, Irene Hachat, Joanne DeGoria, Alice Eckel, Joyce Benson, Nickie Oliver, Carol Dziedzic, Betty Sherman, Georgette Worob and instructional assistants Sue Levine, Cathy Rehwinkel, Samita Bhatia, and Vimla Udeshi.

Thank you for the poetry workshops Jim Haba, Gretna Wilkinson, Peter Murphy and Yousef Koumanyakaa.

Special thanks to Sharon Schlegel, staff reporter, and Cindy DeSau, photographer, of the Trenton Times newspaper, Dr. E. Lama Wonkeryor of AHLP Communications, and Anne Hamilton who introduced me to my publisher.

Special gratitude to comrade quilters Mada Coles Galloway, Cheryl Beckles, Melanie Norman, *Storytellers in Cloth, Turtle Creek Quilters Guild,* The Friendly Quilters and my favorite sources for fabric Tunde Tada, The Quilters' Barn, Pennington Quiltworks and Joanne Fabrics.

Lastly and with longevity, my heartfelt thanks to the very special people, places and institutions that have made me a lifelong learner: Jean Washington of Princeton University's African American Studies program, Dr. Richard and Alice Hope of the Woodrow Wilson Fellowship Foundation, Dr. Don Harris, president emeritus of Alpha Phi Alpha fraternity, The National Sorority of Phi Delta Kappa, Inc., Epsilon Alpha chapter, Dr. Helen Martinson, coordinator of Princeton University's Teachers as Scholars program, New Jersey Education Association, Mercer County Education Association and the 1964 graduating class of East Orange High School, especially Cassandra Lonesome Manuel, Linda Jackson Scott, Janice Harris Jackson, Mary Elizabeth Young, Evelyn Baker, and Shielah Wilson Shareef.

# Who is Nefu Books?

Africana Homestead Legacy Publishers will publish more books for children and literature under its imprint Nefu Books. Look for the first titles in late 2009 and early 2010.

# Forthcoming Nefu Books

*P'nut Butter and Rubber*

*Pick Your Own Time*

*The Tractor Sneaker Flip*

*A Cornfield Maze Escapade*

# Africana Homestead Legacy Publisher imprints

Africana Homestead Legacy Publishers, Inc., has five imprints:

Africana Homestead Legacy Publishers (scholarly nonfiction and literary fiction)

AHLP Books (popular autobiography, biography, and memoirs)

Nefu Books (juvenileand childrens literature)

Oyinde Publishing (inspirational, light fiction, romance, and self-help)

AHLP Communications (scientific, technical, and medical)

# Visions of Black Life

Africana Homestead Legacy Publishers welcomes submissions of poetry and short stories from children, juveniles, and adults for its literary journal, *Visions of Black Life: A Collection of Outstanding Short Stories and Poetry.*

Send manuscripts for consideration to this address:

SAN 914-4811
Africana Homestead Legacy Publishers, Inc.
Attn: VBL Acquisitions
811 Church Road, Suite 105
Cherry Hill, NJ 08002

editors@ahlpub.com

# Buy our books online

You may also buy *Learning English the Cultural Way* and other AHLP titles online.

Amazon at amazon.com

Barnes and Noble at barnesandnoble.com

ABE books at abebooks.com

More choices from booksellers in the Amazon.com marketplace

# License Electronic Rights

You may license the electronic rights for *Learning English the Cultural Way* and other AHLP titles.

Check rights availability and fees at the Copyright Clearance Center:

222 Rosewood Drive
Danvers, MA 01923
USA
Phone: 978-750-8400
E-mail: info@copyright.com
Web site: copyright.com

Send other request to rights@ahlpub.com.

Printed in the United States
142363LV00004B